MW00941992

DETERMINED HEARTS

HEARTS

A FRANKENSTEIN

ANTHOLOGY

FOR MARY

Thank you for two hundred years of Victor Frankenstein and his Creature.

You and your "hideous progeny" have captivated the imaginations and seized the souls of countless dreamers, writers, artists, and kindred spirits.

I hope this little book serves as a reminder of those who will never forget you.

Contents

Introduction

"What can stop the determined heart and resolved will of man?"
—Frankenstein—

Frankenstein's monster first came to life—not with a flash of lighting and a maniacal voice shouting, "It's alive" to the heavens—but through the vivid and passionate imagination of a brilliant young woman.

While on holiday in Switzerland, Mary Shelley took part in a "scary story" contest with her husband and their companions—Lord Byron, Claire Clairmont, and John Polidori.

Although Mary initially struggled to come up with a fitting story, she was intrigued by a discussion of galvanism—the use of electric current to temporarily animate muscle tissue.

According to Shelley's introduction to the 1831 edition of *Frankenstein*, initial inspiration for the story came to her through a horrifying waking dream about a young medical student who built a man and then brought him to life.

Encouraged by her companions to expand her short story into a novel, Mary set to work. The result was *Frankenstein,* first published anonymously in 1818.

Although somewhat overshadowed by its countless re-interpretations, imitators, and parodies, the brilliance of Mary Shelley's original novel still shines through with stunning poignancy and clarity.

The work of the ten creators in this anthology explores how the legacy of Mary Shelley's creation continues to inspire female and gender-fluid writers and artists—even 200 years after *Frankenstein's* initial publication.

One of the many things that struck me when I re-read the novel in preparation for this project was that Victor Frankenstein and his Creation are mirrors of each other, two halves of the same self.

Each character exhibits both compassion and cruelty, and the story suggests that these traits may not contradict each other after all. There can be viciousness, even in kindness. Fundamental human decency remains—even in the most deplorable of perpetrators.

This duality of human nature remains a dominant theme in many of the works you will read in this anthology. As the speaker of "Why Didn't You Create Me from Mechanical Parts?" reflects, humanity is our "tragedy," yet it is also our greatest triumph.

The tragic golem in "Unfinished and Unformed" experiences both the "sweet and the bitter" of becoming more human. The protagonists of "The Seer Witch" and "Lineage" exhibit both unsettling kindness and compassionate brutality, as they cultivate a creative legacy through destruction.

In the poems of Diana Adams, Emma Lee, and Travis Black, the "Creature" mourns both the humanity that has been denied him—and the humanity he experiences all too deeply. Nancy Etchemendy's poem "Monster" addresses Mary Shelley herself, defly identifying the complex psyche that created a Monster and his Maker.

The visual poetry of Amanda Earl and Travis Black's "Weeping Adam" also reflects the tragic duality of humankind. Lines that are simultaneously harsh, and yet gentle create intricate images that are both calming and unsettling.

At one point, the title character of "The Pigeon Woman" observes that even dead things cannot die. Rather, they only take on new forms. The same can be said of human nature—the complexity of which has been beautifully encapsulated through two hundred years of *Frankenstein*.

—*JACQUELINE F DORSEY, EDITOR*—

MONSTER

NANCY ETCHEMENDY

about nancy etchemendy

Nancy Etchemendy's novels, short fiction, and poetry have appeared regularly for the past 25 years, both in the U.S. and abroad. Though she is best known for her children's books, she has also published several dozen stories for adults. She particularly enjoys writing dark fantasy and horror.

Her work has earned a number of awards, including three Bram Stoker Awards (two for children's horror), a Golden Duck Award for excellence in children's science fiction, and an International Horror Guild Award.

She lives and works in Northern California where she alternates identities between an introverted writer of weird tales and the gracious spouse of a Stanford philosophy professor.

Ah, Mary,
the dark vision found you,
as visions do
against your will,
convinced of your freedom
while you slept, curled
in married Percy's arms,
mother of his buried baby,
on the whispering shore
of a lake closer to home
than you thought.

You dreamed of a man sewn from scavenged
parts of the discarded dead as you made your own
life from the wreckage
of your mother's demise, your father's wrath,
the strange mores
of a time suffocated in its bed.

Ah, Mary,
you saw our future
misshapen, lurching
forth from the night,
from steam and alchemy
and lightning stolen from
a sky that once belonged
only to God, impossible
for any but a blind child
to love.

SELECTED WORK

TRAVIS BLACK

about travis black

Travis J. Black is a Michigan artist and poet, who graduated with a professional certificate in Computer Information Systems with a concentration in Web Design from Oakland Community College.

Black, who is gender-fluid, uses art and poetry to expand, experiment, and articulate themes of sexuality, gender, the metaphysics of the soul, and human identity.

WEEPING ADAM

by Travis Black

I, THE DEVIL

I do not have horns
Nor a forked tail
Nor mammalian wings

I do not have a lupine
Snout
Nor cherry red skin

I am a man-
Nothing
More
Nothing
Less

UNFINISHED
&
UNFORMED

LEON CRAIG

about leon craig

Leonora "Leon" Craig Cohen has published stories on *Litro.co.uk,* in Oxford University's *Notes Magazine,* and in the *Next Review.* Her short immersive play *Ermine/Stoat* was produced at Babel Studios Southwark.

Her short story 'Mute Canticle' was shortlisted for the *White Review* short story prize last year. She also won a Young Writer's Award from *theshortstory.co.uk.*

Leon Craig has performed at Polari/LGBTQ History Month, Swimmers, QueerCircle London, That's What She Said, The Moth, and Women's Art for Change. Leon is currently writing her first collection, *Spiteful Tales,* and will be presenting at Brainchild Festival's Short Story Hour in Sussex this summer.

She is particularly interested in writing about queerness, abjection, folklore and the Middle Ages.

Follow her on Twitter *@Leon_C_C*

UNFINISHED & UNFORMED

Emet. Met. Emet. Met. Truth. Death. Truth. Death.

And then, Light. Dark. Light. Dark.

In the beginning these were the only distinctions. Then came sound and silence, movement and stillness.

I had limbs and those limbs were moving. I chopped the wood and brought it in, then I swept the floors.

I had hands. I used my hands to stir the pot and scrub it when it was empty. I had fingers, I held a gray-white bone-handled knife between them to cut up cabbages and onions.

The woman cut the chickens herself, brought them near to the door, hanging by the legs, shrieking and flapping. She stilled them with the little knife.

The blood was collected in a pan at her feet, where it was joined by glossy feathers, their brightness slowly dulling as they sank. She cut out the major veins and threw them on top of the mess. They looked like purple worms the chickens themselves would have pecked excitedly from the ground.

They leaked more blood onto the feathers; I could smell it. It was like the head of the axe with which I used to cut trees in the forest. But I didn't want to put the axehead in my mouth.

She seemed to think when she rubbed the *aleph* from the wax tablet around my neck, that I would be still the way the chickens were still.

I felt her pick me up and put me in the corner of

the room, under a blanket. I could hear the hiss of the broth as the pot kept boiling on the embers of the fire, the birds singing in the trees outside, the stream running past the place where we lived.

She sang in another language I did not yet know, familiar but alien. She spoke in it as well; I could not see if she was reading or reciting.

I could smell her eating the food we had made. She would rub off the *aleph* before sundown one day and scratch it back on some time after sundown the next.

As the days separated out and I began to understand the routines by which we lived, it became clearer that this happened once a week.

Plum trees grew on the plot, dark plums with a silvery-blue fur that was easily scraped off, like the powder from a butterfly's wing. She made me go out with a little stepladder and a woven basket to gather them before they fell.

Instead of eating these, she would put them into large clay pots in the cellar and leave them until they produced a sweet, musty smell, not unlike the plaited bread she baked after I had finished kneading dough.

She would go to the cellar sometimes and poke at these pots with a stick to check on them. Nearby was a store of bottles containing a clear liquid that burnt my mouth and also smelt faintly of plums.

Sometimes when I was dead, she would drink lots of this liquid and cradle me on her lap, rocking me back and forth. Her hands were rough from the work she did, but they still felt small and plump. Because she did not know that I could think, she never knew these were the times I liked best.

She told me that her father was a very wise man, who lived over the mountains. When he sang his holy songs, the animals would stand on their hind legs to listen. Even the *szlachta* respected him and sent emissaries to hear his advice.

He was so pure that the spirits of righteous men who still had tasks to complete on Earth could occupy his body for a time. I wanted to ask if I was a righteous man, but I did not have the gift of speech.

Her father had taught her how to read and write and had chosen not to notice when she read books intended only for learned men—ancient books and new ones, from as far away as Prague.

She told me the story of how she met her Hiram, with his glossy black curls and broad shoulders. He would come to the window of the kitchen to sell ribbons and lace and other things. The servant girl would try to shoo him away, but she was almost as reluctant as her mistress.

He wandered through all the *shtetls*, tracing his route back and forth. Increasingly, he traced back to her, sung new songs to her that nobody who lived nearby had sung her yet. She was promised to a second cousin, kind and also very learned, but the peddler was the only man who interested her.

It became clear she had been too interested in him. Her father married them himself, with two of the poorest men in the settlement as witnesses, and he recited the story of Jacob's flight from the house of Laban. There was no dancing that day.

Despite these Sabbath intimacies, she didn't like me much when I was alive. If I dawdled bringing back the logs, or let the stew burn in the pot, she would smack the back of my head.

It was neither pleasant nor unpleasant, simply a feeling of sudden pressure. No matter how hard she hit, my head would slowly swell back out, erasing the impression of her hand.

Once, she said to me, "Be more careful, you ugly thing! Without a soul, you cannot speak. If you cannot speak, you can't ask questions. So listen when I talk!"

I had not known that I was ugly.

I imagined that I must look like a clay copy of her, with dark brown eyes and a pointed chin. Perhaps she thought that she was ugly?

The next time her clothes were dirty, I went to wash them in the shallow pool nearby. I hadn't thought to study myself before, but I did now.

I was grey and lumpened, with a wide slashed mouth and a broad, crude nose. She had never meant for me to be looked at. I remembered her face and marked the points of difference.

Yet as I watched my reflection flickering on the water, it slowly came to look more and more like her, until I was standing in her image, quite naked on the bank. I wrung out a wet dress and put it on, tucking the wax tablet out of sight.

I was beautiful.

Just then, Nama, the basket-weaver's wife, who lived on the neighbouring plot, came with her own washing.

I'd never seen Nama, though I'd heard her through

the blankets that covered my hiding place when she came round to talk about the settlement. She gave information not as if she wished to share it with my creator, but as if she were unloading part of some heavy burden every time she visited.

"You shouldn't come out here alone. Look at yourself, you're all soaked. When is that husband of yours going to return? Mine came back from town yesterday and they're all saying there's going to be another revolt. The *szlachta* told our collectors to ask for higher rents. He can keep me safe, but what will you do, all alone in that house?"

I stared at her, the hair shoved back under a patterned scarf, the breasts pulling in opposite directions. She had a dark patch beneath each eye. I wasn't sure my new form would hold and had no practice making expressions with another face.

"Do you have anything to tell me?" I moved my new lips, but still could not reply.

"Not a word of thanks! You always were a proud woman. Well, don't expect another warning from me!" She picked up her heap of clothes and went in search of one of the other washing spots.

My face in the water changed again, first to the new face that I'd just learned, then to my original ugliness. Every time I came out to the pool, I changed my face again. Sometimes, I tried to make my face look like one of the chickens, but that never succeeded.

My creator did not like to send me so far out of her sight, fearing that I would be discovered. She herself seldom ventured out of her home. There was enough work to be done inside. The carpets that kept out the cold at night needed to be beaten and scrubbed. Fruits and berries had to be boiled down into preserves and vegetables pickled in salt water.

Eventually, she would need to leave and sell her pots of plums to the tavern keeper, who would transform them into liquid. There were always other things she had to buy because she could not make them, though she had made life itself.

One day as I was sweeping the floor, a brown beetle ran ahead of my broom. I snatched it up and turned my hand so it lay curled in the valley of my palm. Gradually, it stretched out its legs, as fine as hairs and ran up my fingers, climbing as I turned my hand.

I shook it off onto the table and spent the afternoon making it run to and fro, blocking its path and guiding it in smaller and larger circles.

I did not realise it was nearly sunset until my creator was standing over me. She crushed the beetle with her fist and hauled me to my feet. "Hiram is coming tomorrow night and you have wasted the whole day. You are not a child, you were made to work. Get on with it, or I will return you to the dust!"

So, for the first time, I watched her Sabbath observances while she carefully ignored me. At nightfall the next day, she bundled me in two shawls and pushed me out of sight.

When Hiram finally returned, she asked him, "Did you see him? Did you see our son? Is he well?" For the first time, I knew rage. She had *made* someone else before me.

For the next week I lay there listening to the creator and Hiram. They barely left the house, and she fed him all the delicacies we had made. She was his flower, his jewel. He adored her.

He said he was sorry she had to work so hard for so little gain, that fewer people seemed to want his wares each time he passed through. Last year's harvest had been bad, so times were bad for everyone.

She accused him of having another wife, another family, but I did not hear any sound of slapping, and her voice sounded different than it did when she reprimanded me.

It was only after they'd finished laughing that I understood how seldom she had laughed before.

I grew bolder when he was gone.

He had left behind a dark mirror in a carved wooden frame nobody would buy because it had a fracture line in the corner. Whenever my Creator was out of the house, I would sit at the table on the chair and run through her expressions in the glass. I could smile, raise an eyebrow, frown and grimace. Tears were beyond me. I liked to mouth words and pretend that I was speaking.

One morning, she had gone into the woods to gather mushrooms, saying I could not be trusted to choose safely. I ventured to put on her least torn dress and sat brushing out hair that was not mine, admiring eyes that were not mine either. If I had this face, Hiram would love me.

A shout came from the woods, then the sound of something big falling. My Creator ran through the door with leaves and grasses in her hair, so fast that the sight of me stopped her halfway to the cellar.

She grabbed my elbow, as if about to strike me in the mouth for insolence, then looked towards the open door behind her. She threw me halfway across the room and, as I heard the trapdoor in the corner snap closed, I found myself lying on the floor, looking at two brown leather boots thick with filth.

The man had a large, round beard and wore a long loose belted coat. He was talking very fast, and some of his words were the same words the woman used, but I could not understand him. He picked me up and sat on the bed with me resting on his lap, the way she sometimes held me.

The man unbelted his coat and pulled a little flask from the inside pocket, offering it to me before taking a swig from it. He was still talking, but more slowly now.

Without warning, he yanked up my dress to the level of my neck, to put his large hairy hands on her breasts. I was off his lap now and lying on the bed as he let his britches drop. He was breathing in the same way Hiram breathed during the visit. Maybe this was what men did.

He seemed to be searching for something on my body, though as far as I could tell, I had made myself look like her in every particular respect.

The prodding continued, the man was getting more and more annoyed. I knew that the bed should be moving at this point, so I curled my legs around him and hurled myself back a few times. *Was that it?* He grabbed both my shoulders and pushed harder.

My Creator was coming out of the cellar now, silently behind him. She drew the little knife across his throat.

Blood was in my eyes and mouth and on my tongue. When it ran out, I put my lips up to the wound and ate. I crunched the bones and sucked the marrow. I savored the brain and swallowed the organs, slippery and rich. There was not much left of him but shreds of skin.

My creator still held the knife, an expression of disgust on her face. She snatched the amulet from my neck and clutched it in her other hand as if she wished to break it. Sighing, she looked down at the man's big leather boots.

Taking the knife, she scoured along the edges of the wax on each side of the amulet, levering the *emet* and the tetragrammaton from their frames.

She took my chin in her bloodied hand and put the words inside my mouth. These were sweet and bitter going down. I knew now the difference between pain and pleasure. I knew now I could name myself and that one day I would die.

"If Adonai sees fit to give you a soul, perhaps you will understand what it is you've done."

I thanked her and went to put on the Cossack's clothes, after I'd put on his face.

WHY DIDN'T YOU CREATE ME FROM MECHANICAL PARTS?

EMMA LEE

about emma lee

Emma Lee's most recent poetry collection is *Ghosts in the Desert* (IDP, UK, 2015).

She was co-editor of *Over Land, Over Sea: Poems for Those Seeking Refuge* (Five Leaves, UK, 2015) and *Welcome to Leicester* (Dahlia Publishing, UK, 2016).

Emma Lee reviews for *London Grip*, *The High Window Journal*, and *Sabotage Reviews*.

Visit *emmalee1.wordpress.com*.

WHY DIDN'T YOU CREATE ME FROM MECHANICAL PARTS?

To be created human was my tragedy.
Love and beauty I observed and understood
yet knew neither would apply to me.

The loss of your mother drove you to study
reanimation and birth me under night's hood.
To be created human was my tragedy.

Did you think, as you worked stealthily,
that you gave me heart and brain? Yet, you would
behave as if neither would apply to me?

From hiding I watched a loving family,
acted kindly towards them but they misunderstood;
to be created human was my tragedy.

You were betrothed, why not me?
You shrunk from me in fear, in self-pity; could
you see neither would apply to me?

I am monstrous and alone, miserably
so. You destroyed my bride: love and the food
of belonging, you knw neither would apply to me.
To be created human was my tragedy.

THE PIGEON WOMAN

AN EXCERPT FROM THE NOVEL
GOBLIN

EVER DUNDAS

about ever dundas

Ever Dundas is a queer, disabled writer, specialising in the weird and macabre.

"The Pigeon Woman" is a brief excerpt from her debut novel, *Goblin*, published in May 2017 by Freight Books.

LONDON 1937

The Crazy Pigeon Woman of Amen Court walked by our school every morning. If she walked by when we were on break, we'd be at the fence, spitting and shouting.

She'd shuffle along, talking to herself, spit sliding down her back. Soon, we got bored after no reaction every morning. We would just mumble obscenities, shout lazily in her direction. There came a time we didn't notice her at all and spat and shouted at each other instead.

She would always have a troop of pigeons following her along the street. Some of the kids spat on the pigeons too, until I pummelled them.

I spun tales about her magic abilities, that she collected our spit and used it in potions. "She could kill you," I said. "She has your essence. She only has to say the word and you'd drop down dead." The little kids peed their pants, the others told me to fuck off, saying I was as crazy as she was.

I pretended I was the Pigeon Woman of Amen Court, all calm and aloof. Soon, I was the only one left at the fence and I'd watch her and her pigeons.

One morning I saw her hair move, like it was alive, like it could move on its own. "Excuse me," I saids polite as can be, but she walked right by, muttering, scattering seeds.

I jumped the fence and walked by her side, glancing up at her, staring at the little pigeon heads poking out from her mess of hair.

It really *was* a bird's nest, matted here and there, with bits of twig sticking out.

"Are they babies?" I said. "Baby pigeons living in your hair?" She muttered and I leaned in to hear but caught nothing.

She grabbed my hand, and I was ready to pummel her, but I couldn't, not with pigeons in her hair. She dropped seeds in my hand, or tried to. It was all scrunched up in a fist and the seeds just bounced off, scattering.

"You can feed them," she said. "Don't you want to?" She bent a little and I opened my hand, catching the seeds, and I fed the pigeons in her hair.

"We call you Pigeon," I said, trying to be polite, not telling her what we really called her.

"I know what you call me," she said. She wasn't stupid, that crazy pigeon woman.

"Come inside," she said, "and have a cup of tea."

We'd reached her house. I'd left school without really knowing it, and I stared back down the road, and at her troop of pigeons, and in I went.

Animals everywhere, staring, fake.

"Taxidermy," she said.

I didn't know what that meant and screwed up my face in thought.

"I find them," she said, "and I preserve them. I take out their guts and make them like this."

"Like an Egyptian mummy," I said.

She just grunted. I ran my finger along one of the shelves, wanting to touch the mummified animals, but I was nerved by their glassy eyes.

Pigeons walked amongst them, pecking at seeds. Seeds and pigeon shit were everywhere. The smell was strong, a welcoming, musty animal smell.

"Why?" I said.

"Dead things can't die," she said.

I nodded, as if I understood.

"Sit," she said, and I sat. She shuffled off, a small troop following her even in the house.

She brought me some tea and a biscuit. I inspected it for pigeon shit and shoved it in my mouth. "You got more biscuits?"

"You hungry? You can stay for dinner."

I shrugged, sipping my tea. A pigeon scrambled up my leg, its claws digging into me. I let it be, and it stood on my knee, eating seeds from my hand. It settled on my leg, falling asleep, looking up at me suspiciously anytime I moved an inch.

I drank my tea and stared at the Pigeon Woman. I squinted at her, trying to see the pigeons in her hair.

"They're sleeping," she said, seeing me look at her head. "All asleep in their nest. I can feel them, their little warm bodies. He likes you," she said, gesturing at the sleeping pigeon on my knee.

I stroked his head, and he cooed at me. I looked up, not sure if he was happy or annoyed. The Pigeon Woman smiled. "He likes you," she repeated.

"What's that?" I , pointing to a mummified creature next to my chair. I leaned over and stroked its head the way I'd stroked the pigeon, almost expecting it to coo at me too.

"A shrew," she said. I didn't know what to say, so I just stroked the mummified shrew and stared round the room.

There were framed photos everywhere, of what looked like the Pigeon Woman and her family. I didn't pay much attention to the photos, except to notice they were the only things not covered in pigeon shit.

"Do you like stories?"

"Uh-huh."

"I'll tell you stories. I can tell you all about London," she said. "Of the realm below and the realm above." She paused, arching her eyebrow.

"Did you know that lizard people live in the realm below?" I shook my head.

"They hide away in the myriad of tunnels and caves in the depths of London. It's their kingdom,where the Lizard King and Queen rule."

"They eat the big black insects that live there too. They're as big as my hand." She raised her hand, spreading her fingers.

"And the lizard people eat them – *crunch*! Do you know what would happen if they didn't? The insects would multiply and take over the realm below and the realm above."

"Like in the Bible," I said, "in Revelation – 'And there came out of the smoke, locusts upon the earth and unto them was given power, as the scorpions of the earth have power... And they had a king over them, which is the angel of the bottomless pit.'"

"That's right. You understand, don't you?" said the Pigeon Woman, smiling and nodding.

"London would be ruled by these insects, but we have the lizard people," she continued. "They come to the realm above, in the form of humans. But I recognise them, I know them. You can tell by their eyes. They keep their lizard eyes, and they glint emerald, all shades of blue, sometimes red. They come from below and they feed off the rays of the sun. The lizard people," she said, "are demigods. Part-human, part-divine."

"Holy, Holy, Holy."

"Shall I tell you of the realm above?"

"Uh-huh."

"Have you heard of the Queen of Hearts?" she asked, leaning over and raising her eyebrows. "It is said that Queen Isabella walks these streets carrying the heart of her husband. But it's not true. The heart is pinned to her dress like a brooch. It still beats, dripping blood, staining Isabella's dress, leaving a trail on the ground.I've seen her," the Pigeon Woman continued, "she haunts these streets."

SELECTED VISUAL POETRY

ARTISTIC RENDERINGS
OF PASSAGES FROM
FRANKENSTEIN

AMANDA EARL

about amanda earl

Amanda Earl's visual poetry has been exhibited in
Brazil, Russia and Canada and has been published in
Fantagraphics' *The Last Vispo Anthology*.

Her visual poetry chapbook *Of the Body* was
published by Puddle of Sky Press. *A Fieldguide to
Fanciful Bugs* was published online by Avantacular
Press. For more visual poetry, please visit
EleanorIncognito.blogspot.ca.

Amanda is the author of *Kiki* (Chaudiere Books),
the managing editor of *Bywords.ca,* and *The Fallen Angel*
of AngelHousePress. For further information, please
visit *AmandaEarl.com*.

"[These philosophers] have indeed performed miracles. They penetrate into the recesses of nature, and show how she works in her hiding places. They can command the thunders of heaven, mimic the earthquake, and even mock the invisible world with its own shadows."

Frankenstein, Chapter 3

"No one can conceive the variety of feelings which bore me onwards, like a hurricane, in the first enthusiasm of success. Life and death appeared to me ideal bounds, which I should first break through, and pour a torrent of light into our dark world."

Frankenstein, Chapter 4

THE SEER
WITCH

JAMIE LANDRY

about jamie landry

Jamie Landry graduated from the University of Maine at Farmington, with an individualized major in Creative Writing and Art. Her work has been featured in the *Sandy River Review.*

Jamie has always been drawn to the macabre and horrific. This is her first horror story, and she's honored to share her voice with the others in this anthology. Jamie lives and writes with her growing family in Maine.

THE SEER WITCH

"Mrs. Seer," the nurse shook my shoulder. "Mrs. Seer, we need you to wake up."

I opened my eyes to the harsh overhead lighting, and I could make out the fuzzy white paper wings of her hat. I imagined it taking flight like a bird from her head. Flying off to places unknown.

I pictured myself high in the sky, looking down on the terrain, a pattern of landscape stitched together. Houses dotting the wavy tapestry like tiny beads sewn by the most deft hands. I felt the rush of cool ocean air blowing through my feathers.

"Mrs. Seer, you had a baby girl." Through the drugged fog, the words reached me just as I was gliding over enormous, sharp rocks growing straight out of the water and piercing the sky above. "Mrs. Seer, can you hear me? I said, 'You had a baby girl.'"

"Wh-where is she?" I asked, as the ocean I was soaring above froze into green linoleum tiles under fluorescent lights.

I reached out my arms, ready to meet my sweet child. It was then I noticed the solemn look on the nurse's face. She was almost as white as her perfectly starched and ironed uniform.

"Where is she?" The panic strained my voice into a pin dot of sound.

"Mrs. Seer, Dr. Jones thinks it's best if you and Mr. Seer go home and forget you were pregnant. You can try again in a few months." The hint of apology dusted the shape of her words.

"What are you saying?" Anger started to build in my core. "Where is she? Is she dead? Oh, God..."

I felt the blood in my body ice over. A primal wail clawed at the room. The nurse had her hand on my mouth before I knew the scream was my own.

"Shhhhhhh, shhhhhh, Mrs. Seer. She isn't dead. But you don't want to see her." The nurse dropped her hand. I combed through her unspoken words to retrieve what she wanted to tell me.

"Don't tell me what I want. If my baby is alive, you bring her to me. Now!" I yelled at her.

With an exasperated sigh, she left the room. A few minutes later, I was holding the most beautiful creature I'd ever laid eyes on. I couldn't understand why the nurse told me I wouldn't want to see her.

She was perfect. Pink and warm with the tiniest pair of lips. Her tiny hands held onto the hem of the blanket, as though searching for comfort.

I looked at the nurse to ask why she told me those awful things, but her mouth was quicker than mine. "Your baby has a deformity," she said.

The nurse took the baby from my arms, laid her

on the bed and unwrapped her. As the baby let out a pathetic cry, her bottom lip started to quiver.

"Shhhhhhhhhh..." The nurse stuck an index finger in the baby's little mouth as she let me study her dainty body: fragile arms, skinny belly, the umbilical cord still yellow with the last meal she had inside me, the diaper impossibly small, but still too large for her.

Then my eyes found two buds where her legs were supposed to be. Like two sprouts barely pushed through the soil before the frostbitten hands of winter wrapped around them, choking the life from their pure, tender stems.

"I highly doubt you and Mr. Seer want to bring home a freak." I don't remember throwing a punch, only the way her eye felt as it popped against my knuckles.

The heartbreaking memory started to fade, as I woke on the morning of Adeline's eleventh birthday to starlings sending up their voices into the bright blue sky. The cool October air swept through the open window running its fingers over my face, as gentle as a lover.

I rolled over to the side of the bed that used to belong to my husband, but for the whole of Adeline's life, had remained empty. He left when she was barely a week old.

I was happy to see him go. The way he looked at Adeline when I handed her to him. It wasn't disgust churning in those death-black pupils. It was disappointment, and it filled the void left in my womb. A few days later, he left, justifying his departure with a claim that he was "cursed."

"The war came home with me. Too many lives hang around my neck, Bel. I'm not meant to be happy after everything I've done. You and Adeline shouldn't be haunted by my demons."

He stood by the front door with his suitcase. His thin frame made even more hollow by the orange light slipping through the glass and touching his edges. I held Adeline close as I stared at the man getting smaller and smaller in front of me.

He walked forward to kiss Adeline. "Get out," I said, stepping back from him.

"Annabel, at least let me kiss her goodbye."

"Don't," I shook my head, as anger pulsed through my fingers and I began to throw the contents of our house at him. Adeline started to wail, echoing my own anger, and magnifying it tenfold.

Once I'd stopped screaming, I looked up and saw that the beautiful stained glass window I loved so much was now splintered as my own ragged heart. I fell to the floor, bits of yellow and orange glass glittering in the last caress of the sun's rays.

I touched my eyes; no tears, no anguish threatening to suck me into a black hole of despair. It was relief that washed over me in gentle waves. Adeline curled into me; we slept all night together.

I awakened the next morning to a neighbor nailing boards over the holes in our windows. If I had known the boards would still be there eleven years later, I would have asked him to be a little neater.

That night—that one cathartic blink of psychosis—forever changed me in the eyes of my neighbors. That very night, a whisper begin to slither around the village like a python.

At first, people felt sorry for me. A woman giving birth to a freak, and on Halloween no less. And her husband walking out on her at almost the same time. Gradually, they began to turn against me.

She really should try to sort herself out, that one. Can't dwell on the past. Everyone has something awful happen to them.

Then when odd events and disappearances occurred, the villagers finally spoke their tiny, useless minds.

She's a witch. Never comes out, neither does that freak daughter of hers. I heard she cut the legs off that poor baby to give to the devil himself. Her soul wasn't worth enough to him as it was. She needed to chop those tiny little legs off that poor, helpless baby to make up the difference.

Oh, they had no idea how tame the devil was, compared to me. The things I'd relished doing would sicken that horned beast to the crater of his soul.

The villagers sat in their small houses with their small minds, waiting for tantalizing glimpses of Adeline and me.

Our hulking Victorian was the only home of its kind. Brick from the ground up, its dominant features were the black trim on roughly-nailed windows—and the intact bits of stained glass peeking through Tangled coils of ivy were slowly taking over the house's facade— each fresh strand pulling us closer to Hell.

As I lay under the warmth of my covers, I suddenly remembered that it was Adeline's birthday and quickly sprung into action. I threw back the bed covers, letting the October air wrap its icy fingers around my body. I grabbed my robe.

I loved this day even more than Adeline did. It was the one day each year that I could give her exactly what she wanted.

I stepped into the hallway, carefully avoiding the boards that squeaked whenever an absentminded foot touched them. The floors had been stunning once. They were made of rich mahogany with a whisper of red that blazed like the embers of fire. Even if I scrubbed the floor for days, I don't think I'd ever get rid of the layers of rusty black blood that were now embedded there.

My hand glided down the banister, following that thick snake of timber, anticipating every nick and scratch before they ran under my fingers. As they revealed their splintered bellies, I remembered how each nick came to be.

There was Gregory, the boy who had greeted me at the door with a pipe from his father's hardware store. After I had wrestled it from his gangly prepubescent hands, I slammed it into his head.

Charlotte, the girl who pretended to be Adeline's friend so she could steal her wheelchair. I slid her temple onto the delicious spike of the stairpost.

That little Sanderson shit who tried to sneak in and cut a lock of Adeline's hair. I stabbed his neck with metal shears. I left him pinned there for days before I finally yanked the handles out of the wood.

I looked to the left and fingered the wallpaper, a shimmering silver with a red-flocked damask print. It was another reason I loved the house. I'd never seen wallpaper dance in the light the way these walls did. Dried blood trails now licked their forked tongues through the pattern like salacious lovers. I missed the conventional beauty of the house, but the elegance of darkness suited me far better.

I procceded to the kitchen, where horror graced every corner of the room—mallets, frying pans, knives, rolling pins—all stained with the lives of those so eager to take Adeline's. Every year on her Halloween birthday, they would break in on a dare.

C'mon Tommy, don't be a pussy. Kill the bitch. Just stab her in the heart with your dad's bowie knife. Don't you want Mary to like you? She definitely will if you kill the Seer Witch and that freak of hers.

For years, I thought a life cast out from society was the worst despair imaginable. That was until I witnessed people's true capacity for hatred. Their cruelty dragged canyons through my heart. Their viciousness may have been limitless, but it was no match for my own.

After pouring myself some tea, I found Adeline reading. Her hair glowed like a strawberry moon in the sunlight, as her tiny frame bent over the beautiful words that eased her soul.

"Happy birthday, sweet girl." I kissed her head.

"Morning Mum," she said, her eyes locked on the pages before her.

"You might want to find another place to read." I looked out the window and met the prying eyes of a neighbor's child, whose name I'd forgotten. They couldn't pass up one opportunity to gawk at the Freak and the Witch.

I stared back at the child, wishing I had the kind of power they were so convinced I had. I imagined crushing his head, willing the bones to collapse under my gaze.

On the night of Adeline's fouth birthday, the entire village had stood outside the house for hours. In my mind, I can still hear them chanting, "Burn the witch; kill the freak; burn the witch; kill the freak."

I shook off the memory and refocused my attention on the beautiful girl in front of me. "Adeline, you can read upstairs. You know today of all days isn't safe." I placed my hands on the back of her wheelchair, ready to wheel her away.

"But, it's so nice here. Ahhhhhhhhhhhhhhhhhh!"

Glass shattered underneath her scream and rained over the entire room. Adeline pressed her hands to her eyes, her fresh face mangled with shards.

The neighbor I'd seen earlier stood on the sidewalk. His slingshot was still aimed at Adeline. His face was now branded into my mind: cocky dark eyes, defiant stance, a twisted grin on his freckled face.

Oh, I couldn't wait to kill him.

I wheeled Adeline to the bathroom, snapped on the dusty, blood-spattered light, and removed the tiny glass slivers with a needle. I wasn't as careful as I should've been. Those thin red lines made beaded droplets of blood, creating miniature constellations on her face. She winced as I dabbed the cuts with iodine.

"You're as good as new." I cupped her cheeks in my hands.

Her eyes were so weathered. Those eyes had seen nothing but hate from the outside world. She had changed forever the first time she encountered one of the beastly village children.

At five years old, she had believed pixies lived in the flowers. She took several pieces of bread thick with jam and settled amongst the poppies in our garden.

She sat there patiently waiting for the fairies, looking around frantically each time she thought she heard the papery quiver of wings. The shadows of poppies danced across her skin. The blue of her hollow shorts melted into the dirt underneath.

I watched from the kitchen window, until I left to change the sheets on our beds. As I heard a scream rip open the silence, I dropped the sheets and rushed to her side.

I found Adeline, crushed like a petal in the tangle of poppies and innocence. I picked her up, her face covered in blood, inlets of tears cutting through the red, her two front teeth knocked out.

"Mum, w-why does everyone h-hate me so m-much?" Her small voice, so fragile, like the tweet of a bird.

I felt hatred rise in me as I smoothed back Adeline's shining copper hair. "Oh, sweet girl. They don't hate you. They hate themselves."

"W-well it do-doesn't feel li-like it," she stumbled over her sobs.
"Oh, believe me, honey. It's true."

"Th-then why don't they hurt th-themselves?"

"Because, baby, it's easier to cast hate outwards

than it is to accept hate that lies within."

"Well, I ha·hate them. I hate th·them all. A·and I h·hate me too. I ha·hate not ha·ving l·legs. They're r·right. I am a fr·freak."

Up until that point, I had stifled my temper. I lived like the soft, curling smoke of a candle just before it disappeared into nothing—inconsequential and insignificant, only noticeable for a few beautiful seconds before swallowed up by the atmosphere.

But in moments like these, I became both the candle and the flame. Those worthless assholes had ruined my sweet little girl. She hated herself as much as they did. And I hated them all for it.

I wanted to claw off their faces. Hair and nails and blood and skin flying into the air like leaves on the wind. I would be the winter—freezing the life from their branches.

From that point onward, I no longer hunched my shoulders in apology for what we were. No longer would I let the villagers make me their prey. They should have known better than to create their own monster. I delighted in seeing the same flicker burn within Adeline.

As I was swiftly drawn back into the present, I studied Adeline's wounded, vengeful face in the bathroom mirror. "Would you like *him* for your eleventh birthday?" I asked, as I ran my thumb over the dried blood of her scar.

"Yes."

"Then him it shall be."

I turned on my heel and walked to the back porch. I was afraid it was too late, but he was standing in the backyard, still holding that damned slingshot. I had expected him to run, but he just stood there, taking in my lackluster appearance.

No black flowing robes, no hairy moles, no long gray hair. Nothing of the Grimm fairytales or the schoolyard rumors he'd expected. I looked as normal as his mother.

I walked until I was close enough to count the freckles on his cheeks. His pupils shrunk into dots barely big enough to pass a needle through. That young face, so fresh with hate woven into his heartstrings. His was the face of every villager at every second of Adeline's life.

"You hurt my Adeline on her birthday. You're going to come inside and apologize to her." I put my hand on the back of his neck and dragged him inside.

Adeline watched as I snapped his neck. The bones cracked, grinding the gears of his heart to a halt. His head flopped, and his body crumbled to the floor.

It was unsatisfying to have it over so quickly and painlessly. But I knew death was not the end of his torment. Adeline and I could take our time and savor this next moment.

"Adeline, get my knife," I said as I bent over the nameless corpse.

Adeline returned from the kitchen, the blackened knife clenched in her teeth. As she walked on her hands, the pink hem of her dress picked up dust and hair and bone fragments.

"Do you want me to help you, or do you want to do it by yourself?"

Adeline rested herself beside the body. "I want to do it myself."

She drew the blade in a straight line across the boy's lap, a line that showed exactly where the normal and unnatural met. A line she herself could only cross on her birthday. Warm blood pooled around her with welcoming arms

She worked the knife back and forth, its jagged teeth cutting deeper into the marrow. She paused periodically, pressed her hand to her forehead and left bright crimson smudges on her skin that soon faded to rusty brown. Our veins ran with the mud of the Earth.

The wet, meaty sound of her sawing through one leg, then the other, lasted for hours. His dead flesh rolled unchecked under the pull of the blade and the strength of her arms.

When she had severed the last tendon from the torso, she looked up at me with more happiness than I thought could fill those inky blue eyes. Then she cut the pant legs off and removed the clunky shoes. She sat back to admire her gift.

"I'll be right back."

I returned with my camera and a leg brace fashioned from the bottom of an old mannequin.

I carefully slid the dead boy's legs into their mechanical cage. I pushed the cage to the room's center, stopping in front of the snaking banister.

"Are you ready?" I turned to Adeline once everything was in place. She nodded and raised her arms for me to lift her on top of the caged legs. Her dress was stained brown with dried blood—and with bright red blood still dripping from the hem.

I stood back to see my beautiful girl standing on pale legs. I raised the camera, eager to see the photo grow in the red glow of a chemical bath. Eager to add this photo to our growing collection.

I pressed the camera's shutter. "Happy birthday, my sweet Adeline."

LINEAGE

DENISE JOHNSON

about denise johnson

Denise Johnson, an Arizona-based writer is the author of several short stories and film and television scripts. Her film script *Love, Take Two* placed third in the Writer's Digest 84th annual writing competition.

A full-time writer and editor for an insurance news website, she has written over one thousand articles on topics relating to insurance. She received the 2016 Azbee Award for her online feature article "How Wearable Devices Could Disrupt the Insurance Industry."

Denise is particularly interested in writing mystery, horror, and science fiction.

LINEAGE

The blade slowly pierced her stomach. Jan could feel the metal go deeper and deeper as she began to tremble. She was going into shock, she guessed.

Despite the excruciating pain, she smiled. She could see this was unsettling Joe, her oldest child by two minutes. Though Joe was a disappointment to her, it didn't matter now.

She would die fulfilled because Jeff, Joe's twin, had not failed her. She tried to tell Jeff how happy he had made her but could only spit up blood as she gasped for air.

The blood stuck to her long silver hair. Jeff stood in between his mother and his brother, the bloody butcher knife hanging heavy in his hand.

As she clung between life and death, she recalled the day she made the decision. It was after repeatedly being taunted in high school, to the point that she had contemplated suicide. Stuck in the house one summer because her doped-up mother refused to let her out, she rummaged through some old things in the attic.

A yellowed envelope with the return address of a prison fell out of an old book. It was addressed to her mother and postmarked 1974. She would have been five years old at the time the letter was written.

Sitting on an old, rusted mattress frame, she learned that the letter was from her father. Jan's mother never talked about her father, never really told her anything about him. After reading the letter, Jan learned why.

He was in prison for several counts of murder and had been sentenced for life.

When Jan confronted her mother about the letter a few weeks later, her mother attempted to dissuade Jan from visiting her father.

That was confusing. For as long as Jan could remember, her mother had been a pothead with little concern for anyone but herself. Jan began pushing and shoving her mother, as she had seen plenty of men do.

Her mother, scared and crying, finally relented and gave Jan all of the information she needed to make contact with her father.

That same day, Jan sent him a letter to ask if they could meet. Within a week of receiving her letter, he wrote back, inviting Jan to the prison.

With his round glasses and salt-and-pepper hair, Jan's father loocked and acted more like a chemistry professor than a mass murderer. He even offered her advice on dealing with the bullies at school.

She asked him about the murders, and he told her everything. She knew why he murdered, how he did it and the feeling he got with each kill.

The longer her father was in prison, the more depressed he got. He knew he would never be able to kill again. Jan wanted desperately to help.

They talked of breaking him out but no plan seemed plausible. He told her he had another idea. He wanted to prolong his legacy with a grandchild.

At the time, Jan was only 16 and hadn't been with a boy yet. She told her father this and he explained that it didn't matter and that he would find her someone appropriate.

The next week, Jan found herself in a room alone with another serial killer. The conjugal visit lasted only 15 minutes, but it was enough to render her pregnant with twins..

The pregnancy was hard; carrying twins meant several months of bed rest. Mortified at the thought of her daughter carrying a murderer's children, Jan's mother kicked her out.

Homeless and seven months pregnant, Jan moved in with her unborn children's aunt. No matter how sick she felt, she kept up the visits to her father.

Her father gave her letters from other inmates. Most of the letters described killings in detail. He wanted her to read them out loud to the babies. As soon as she could, Jan took Jeff and Joe to see their grandfather. She wanted them to have a strong male presence in their lives.

Jan could see evil in the boys as they grew older. They chased and stomped on all kinds of bugs, birds too. She encouraged them to practice on bigger animals. After starting school, the twins were often sent home for beating classmates.

Jan was happy with their progress, until one day Joe came home crying. He had been sent to the principal's office for repeatedly tripping the same little girl. She ended up with a broken nose and a black eye.

Rather then sending him home, the principal—a nosy know-it-all whom Jan disliked—had asked Joe why he had tripped the girl.

He told her that he had to follow in his dad's and granddad's footsteps and become a bad man. Questioned further, he admitted that he was to be a murderer when he grew up. Without showing any apparent fear, the principal explained the concept of nature versus nurture and said that Joe could be anything he wanted.

Jan seethed with anger at Joe's relucance to fulfill his destiny, so she focused her energy on Jeff instead. She tried to keep the twins separate as much as possible, even giving up her room and sleeping on the couch.

As they grew older, the twins would periodically ask Jan the reason why they couldn't play together, and she would tell them separately that each had an illness the other shouldn't catch.

When they were about to start high school, she knew she wouldn't be able to keep the lie going much longer so she got her mother to agree to let Joe live with her.

As she stared at the knife lodged in her chest, Jan didn't understand why they were together now, after being seperated for years. She had groomed Jeff. Joe hadn't made the cut.

Jeff could see his mother's life ebbing away and that made him happier than he had ever been.

Yes, she had groomed him to be a murderer, and he knew that yearning would be hard to give up. But Joe had promised to help him, free him from the fate his mother tried to seal for him.

That freedom came seconds later when the bullet pierced his brain.

about diana adams

Based in Edmonton, Alberta, Diana Adams has been published in a variety of journals including *Boston Review, Drunken Boat, Fogged Clarity, Oranges & Sardines,* and *The Laurel Review.*

Diana has published three poetry collections:*Cave Vitae* (Plainview Press, 2008), *Theatres of the Tongue* (BlazeVox, 2008), and *Hello Ice* (BlazeVox, 2011).

Her poems have been included in several anthologies including the *Rhysling Anthology (2009)* and *Best American Experimental Poetry* (2016).

Diana is also the author of *To The River,* the first in a three-novella sequence.

SELECTED POEMS

DIANA ADAMS

FRANKENSTEIN'S ICE MIRROR

The left orb protrudes
but the right's a diamond
that captures riverwords,
dwells on velvet faces,
on turned earth and chittering trees.
My hands, stitched, ill-fitted,
forget so many things.
Still, you should love me,
all the words I've learned,
Gull-gray, silent ice—
their echoes attach,
bind you to me.

FRANKENSTEIN, UNDER THE ELM

I carry my thug legs
to the theater of birds and enter
the skin of spiders. Climb boats
of leaves, eat bottle-blue flies,
I try to root in a rabbit's chest,
or drop on summer's floor (ground opens,
lends me a chair in dirt's kitchen).
But I'm so far beyond creatures.
Each stolen, callow eye waters,
bones nestle in alleys
of flesh, my long arms gather
air's soft sugar.

acknowledgements

First, thank you to all who have shared their powerful art, poetry, and fiction.

Thank you to my advisor, Marshall Warfield, for guiding me through the daunting, yet thrilling process of putting this collection together.

Thank you to Susan DiGironimo for showing me the ropes of Adobe InDesign.

Thank you to my copyediting team for going through this manuscript and helping me polish and perfect the book in your hands now.

Thank you to my family for all of their love and support. I certainly could not have made it this far without their encouragement.

Finally, thank you to Mary Shelley, whose *Frankenstein,* a story that is just as haunting—in every sense of the word—today as it was two hundred years ago.

81710728R00048

Made in the USA
Lexington, KY
20 February 2018